SCARS

Nadia Bruce-Rawlings

D1569513

PUNK HOSTAGE PRESS

SCARS
Nadia Bruce-Rawlings

© Nadia Bruce-Rawlings (2014)

ISBN-1940213002
ISBN-1978-1-940213-00-2

Punk Hostage Press
P.O. Box 1869
Hollywood CA, 90078
www.punkhostagepress.com

Editor: Iris Berry

Introduction: Michele McDannold

Cover Layout: Shane Nagel

Cover Photo: Geoff Cordner

EDITOR'S ACKNOWLEDGMENTS:

When A. Razor and I started Punk Hostage Press in 2012, our main goal was to publish books that we could bring into jails, institutions, juvenile facilities, homeless and battered women shelters. Places where books are hard to get, but most needed. Books that could make a difference, inspire and serve as a message that hope is not lost, and there is a way out for a new and better life. I am proud to say that this book you are holding in your hands is actual proof of that very message.

Nadia Bruce-Rawlings has written a collection of stories with a dark humor and candor that only someone with a survivor's gratitude can. She takes us on a journey that cracks open family secrets, illustrating the evolution of dysfunction from its very core. She reminds us, as children we do not get to choose our surroundings, while relying on our parents for protection, love, and nurturing, preparing us for our own adult journey into the world, and that more times than not, this isn't the case. Because parents get abused and scarred, by their parents who got abused and scarred, by their parents, and so on. And with each generation the trauma grows, becoming a collection and a reflection of an ongoing tradition of generational abuse.

This book is written based on Nadia's experiences on the front lines of her own personal battles with child abuse, domestic violence, molestation, addiction, crime, cutting, incarceration, and recovery. After hitting a bottom so hard with only two options left, life or death. Nadia drives home the sad and brutal truth that not everyone gets that choice. Many do not live to tell. This book is written for them, an epitaph. This book is also a love letter and a promise that there is hope for a better life, written for the ones that are still out there, still fighting their way in, and not out, who have lost their way, and still collecting scars.

Punk Hostage Press would like to thank Nadia Bruce-Rawlings for giving us the opportunity and the honor of publishing her first book and trusting us with her words, and her powerful and important message.

I would like to thank A. Razor, my partner and Co-Founder of Punk Hostage Press, without his support, and inspiration this book would not be possible.

We would like the thank Geoff Cordner for his generosity, allowing us to grace the cover of this book with his compelling photograph, one of many from his phenomenal collection and body of work. And Shane Nagel for his generosity of time and talent, designing the cover art.

We would also like to thank Michele McDannold who has been a part of the Punk Hostage Press family since the beginning. For writing such a beautiful and moving Introduction with great love and dedication, as with everything she does. And for our deep friendship that has been sealed while building the foundation of this Press.

With great affection, we would like to thank our families, loved ones, and dearest friends. All of our Punk Hostage Press writers currently and those on deck, and our community of writers and supporters for their on going love and encouragement.

~ Iris Berry 2014

AUTHOR'S ACKNOWLEDGMENTS

I would like to thank my mother, France Bruce, for telling me to never let go of my dreams and for being my guardian angel.

Sophia Bruce for telling me it is never too late and for always believing in me.

Brian Rawlings for loving all my scars.

Geoff Cordner for getting me sober and for his photographs.

Denise Cordner for her love and support through it all.

Courtney, Joshua, Noah and Elijah Rawlings for their tremendous creativity and love and support.

Darby Walker-Curts and Marilyn Moore for always standing by me – I love you two so much.

Michele McDannold for taking me under her wing and guiding me through my first public reading and for the amazing introduction.

Punk Hostage Press; to A. Razor, and to Iris Berry whom I have admired from a distance for decades (when she first told me that I, "write phenomenally," I secretly burst into fan-girl tears) - Thank you for believing in this book and for so patiently walking me through the process.

~ Nadia Bruce-Rawlings 2014

INTRODUCTION

Everybody knows it's best not to talk about it. That awkward moment when you tell a new friend or lover just why it is you are the way you are or you've done the things you've done... thought the things you've thought. These are uncomfortable facts for the person holding them, let alone anyone else. Shame permeates the landscape of an adult dealing with abuse from their childhood. *Don't use it as an excuse*, they say. *You have to move on.* In other words, *forget it.*

Scars is a reminder. Though they fade through time, how they got there never changes. You can make up other stories. You can pretend they're not there. You can douse the memories in one addiction or another, warping the present right along with the past. Still, even in the dark--the raised, rough skin of a scar won't be denied.

Only a brave, beautiful soul could yield so eloquently on the page... to the raw truth of despair, survival, and finally--triumph. Nadia Bruce-Rawlings is one such person. The following pages will evoke a range of emotions. You may feel disturbed. If you have a heart at all, you're going to cry--one of those consuming, cleansing cries that we all need now and then. On the other side, we come to a deeper understanding... and for many, perhaps, not an appreciation but an acknowledgment--a sweet acceptance--of all our scars.

~ Michele McDannold
Author of - *Stealing the Midnight from a Handful of Days*

This Book is Dedicated to my Sweet Sophia

TABLE OF CONTENTS

"Scars have the strange power to remind us that our past is real."

~ Cormac McCarthy

FLOWERS FROM WALMART

He bought her flowers from Walmart

bruised eye, fractured wrist

no groceries again

bottles behind the couch

cat litter's dirty, and the neighbors

grow weary of the noise

baby keeps grinning, but the boy

has a cut on his back

and a scar in his heart

paint's all powder-blue and peeling

chipped in where the dog got kicked

maybe it's just a poem she's waiting for, but

he bought her flowers from Walmart again

and she cried.

FIRE

The day he got out of prison, I went up to Tehachapi to pick him up. It was so hot, and the family members had to wait for what seemed like days before their men were released. Mostly it was married couples, and they stared at me when the old man came out, limping and sweating. Their husbands had done time for drugs or burglary...here I was picking up an old pervert that I just wanted to disown. I didn't want to be there, but he had no one else, and the State needed him to be stable and to register, and so I said yes.

The engine of the truck was still pinging in the heat when we finally got in. He had his bag of belongings and court papers. I didn't hug him, just punched his thin arm and opened the creaky door for him. He looked older than I expected. I hadn't seen him in years, but I didn't think he'd be so grey. The crinkles around his eyes had grown into furrows. I remembered sitting on his lap, didn't seem so long ago, and tracing the little lines with my growing fingers. He always had me sit on his lap, especially when company was there. He'd call me his little girl, and before Mama got sick, she'd smile and shoo me away and sit there herself. Her way of protecting me.

I turned the key and tried to hold the burning stick-shift, and off we went to my place in Bakersfield. It was close enough that I could have visited him every week, but I never brought myself to do that. He wrote letter after letter trying to explain, swearing he was innocent, but I couldn't...he may be my daddy, but I hated his cold, disgusting heart. He turned on the radio to quell the silence, but only the AM worked...men droning on about Jesus and redemption as we drove the 58 into Bakersfield and finally picked up a country station. Daddy used to play guitar, better than most of these guys.

"When do you have to register, Daddy?" I asked as we neared our street. "Should we go today, get it over with?"

He looked at me and just shook his head. "Don't worry about it, I'll get it done."

I shook my head too, but there was no arguing with him. Grown man, gonna do what he was gonna do. Part of me didn't care – let them take him back. The first time, I was almost able to believe his innocence. In his letters he said it wasn't his fault, the little girl had sat on his lap, and when he got excited she had touched it by mistake…like when I was five, till Mama noticed and pushed me off. I didn't know it was wrong, didn't even know it was part of him, but when he got so quiet I knew something wasn't right. Anyway, it was all fine after then, like I said, till Mama died. But his letters sort of convinced me. I mean, the little girl didn't know.

Daddy was gone for just a year then, and it was probably the best time of my life. That's when I moved to Bakersfield, and got the little house I'm still in. No one knew about anything there, and I'd sometimes even venture out to a club to hear a band and see some guitar playing. Daddy played too, like I said, and he was real good. If he wasn't too drunk he'd play old country tunes and Mama'd sing real low. She sounded a bit like Emmylou Harris, and I loved those nights.

Bakersfield was hot and quiet, and I kept to myself mostly. I got Daddy's letters. Sometimes I read them, but I'd save them up for the right time. Couldn't stand his words on just any day. I would sit on the faded couch that had come with the house, and drink a little gin and open them one by one, in date order. The first year in, he just talked a blue streak about being innocent and such. The second time in wasn't so easy; he had to be in solitary most of that run, or he'd be dead. The letters from his second stint were filled with self-pity and denial and made me sick to my stomach. He said he'd found Jesus in there, for a while, but that seemed to fade away as the years went on. By the time he was ready to come home, his letters were mostly rambling dreams of things he wanted to do on the outside.

When he came out this time, I'd already lived in Bakersfield for almost seven years. I didn't really have any friends – some people from work, maybe we'd get a drink once and a while on Country Night, but that was it. I fed the old dog that hovered around out back – his left leg all crooked, but he got by well enough. He never came in, but he did have the nerve to bark once in a while when I hadn't put out water. For Daddy's homecoming I'd put a fresh cloth on the kitchen table. That was as much of a fuss as I was going to make. He'd be gone soon enough if he didn't register anyway. I don't think they were fooling around this time – the little boy he'd touched had been plenty scared and plenty vocal. The parents were at every parole hearing. I was surprised they'd let him out, but I could see how he looked so old and frail now, hardly seemed like he could hurt a flea.

I remember Mama crying a lot when I was young, but she tried so hard to hide it. She kept him away from me after that time she saw me on his lap. But when she got sick with the cancer, things started changing. He loved her, I knew, we all could tell, but I swear the devil was in him when he drank. So he tried to stay sober when she got sick. He even went to AA meetings, and brought home that blue book and chips for 30 days and the whole bit. I was super proud of him, really, and I know Mama was too, what little she understood in her morphine-haze. Then he started working his steps, he called it, and that's when things got bad again. He came home one night just bombed out of his head, tried to hide it from us. He played guitar on the front porch, but kept screwing up all the chords, and then he came in my room. By then I was big, but still scared of his power and his whiskey breath and scratchy beard, and I ran, but he punched and threw me to the ground, and as I felt the fire between my legs, I looked up and saw Mama in the hallway crying on her knees. She didn't last long after that; one morning before dawn I heard silence and knew her breath had stopped and saw blood in the corners of her lips, and her eyes were an empty shell, and next thing I really knew we were burying her down at the church yard.

Daddy kept drinking after Mama was gone, but he stayed away from me – couldn't even look at me anymore. It wasn't long after that he went down for the first time, pled to lewd conduct and away he went. I went to his trial because Mama'd taught me to always keep up appearances, it's what you did. "Keep sunflowers on the table, tea in the fridge and a smile on your face," she'd say, her dark hair shining and her blue eyes so sad. When he came out the first time he'd found a halfway house and a job and the whole bit...looked like he might just be a new man. But he started drinking again, and before I knew it there was a phone call, and he was back in. By then I was in Bakersfield and didn't go to the trials or write or visit. He ended up in CCI, so close to me, but I couldn't dream of letting his cold grey eyes touch mine ever again.

Now here he was, in my truck. We were pulling up to the house, and I had the shivers for a moment. At least no one in town would know his story; no one would look at me in that pitying way when they saw us together.

"Nice place, baby-girl. You done well for yourself," he smiled a bit, trying to be the proud daddy. I just waved him in and grabbed his bags.

"This is your room, Daddy; I'll put your stuff here." I put the bag on his bed, a small twin I'd gotten from up at the Goodwill, but I figured it was better than the slab of cement he was used to at Tehachapi. I'd tried to make it nice and comfy with a homemade blanket and soft pillows. The walls were bare – didn't know if he would still want a cross up on the wall or if he'd gone back to the devil. Time would tell I supposed.

"Want some sweet tea, Daddy?" He nodded yes, and so off I went to my little kitchen with its brand new tablecloth that shamed me just a little.

"I expect you'll want some TV and home cooking...just sit down there, Daddy. I'll make us some supper..." I wanted to keep talking to fill the silence but nothing sounded right. I had decided to grill some steaks and corn to treat him tonight; then we'd go back to plainer fare the rest of the week. I knew he'd be able to get food stamps, but it'd be some time with the paperwork. I didn't want him to get used to me supporting him, that was sure.

My crooked little dog sniffed at the grill hoping for some scraps, but I shooed him off tonight. I was nervous and wanted some gin, but I didn't want Daddy to be drinking. Too late, I saw he'd already found my bottle, and was tipping us both a drink.

So we sat in awkward silence, broken only by chewing and sipping and the occasional small talk. What do you say to someone who's just gotten out of years in the pen? I asked stupid questions about how he felt to be out, and he obliged with stupid answers. Finally I cleared the table, and we turned to the TV for some help. The news was on, and we sipped our gin. Outside grasshoppers and my old dog sniffed around, but otherwise just another quiet night in Bakersfield. I had gotten up early for the drive over to CCI, and I felt my eyes heavy.

Suddenly, he leaned over and stroked my hair, his grey eyes bleary and wet from the gin and the night. I felt his hand touch my breast, and I jumped.

"Daddy, go to bed." And with that I went to my room. I'd been smart enough to install a lock, and once I was safe inside I changed in the dark, listening for his footsteps, his breath, anything. My heart was beating, so fast and hard, and I felt sick to my stomach. I wanted to cry but didn't want to give him that power. Finally I heard the couch creak and his slow shuffle to his room. "Good night, baby-girl."

He woke up before me; guess prison time does that to a man. I got coffee and went to the garage and found it. Last night I'd planned, and I knew I had some. He was quiet and peaceful and looking frail. Old man...sick fuck.

It was almost 8 am when I decided the time was right. We'd hardly said two words to each other. I couldn't, couldn't think of the right thing, the last thing to say. He was at the kitchen table, sipping his coffee and staring into space, and I took some dog food out to the back as an excuse. The garage door was open a bit, but it creaked, and I held my breath. Not a movement from the kitchen though. I grabbed the red container and the lighter and came back in the house. I knew it would burn down, I knew it would all go up, but I didn't care anymore. Last night had taken its toll. I thought he was done, thought maybe he'd changed. But when he touched my breast on the couch everything had flashed back to me. I knew he would never stop, that he hadn't changed a bit.

I was behind him, and every movement was suddenly in slow motion. My head was buzzing, like I'd had too much gin, but I knew what I was doing as I poured the kerosene onto his hair, his shoulder, as he sputtered and screamed, and I lit the lighter and watched it flare.

On the way to the door I picked up my work bag and locked the door behind me, locking in the screams and the crackle. As my neighbor pulled out of her drive way, I smiled, and I waved.

JESUS IN HER HEAD

She talks to Jesus in her head all day. He holds her hand through the hard days, but for a while she couldn't feel him with her. She was one of those lost sheep they talk about. She tried NA but they wouldn't let her talk about Jesus; that made her sad. Sometimes she still goes for the colorful tags they give at 30, 60, 90 days. She has her speech all planned for her one year anniversary. She'll mention Jesus then; what're they gonna do, tear her away from the podium?

At church on Fridays and Sundays she's always right in front, near the band. She gets on her knees right on the floor, her dress rising just a bit too high, but she tries to pull it down as she raises her arms up to Jesus to hold. He holds her tight while she sings and prays and cries. She remembers how the heroin drowned those feelings away. When she smoked it with speed she forgot about her family, she forgot about Jesus, and she let the Enemy into her heart. She was smoking pot by 10, and when her daddy

touched her, then she started with whisky, but that didn't work because the grownups could smell it. The social worker knew the first time he came to interview her that she'd been drinking. He blamed her, told her daddy, and started another round of pain and sorrow. So, she found something that didn't smell. Oxy was first but it was too expensive after a while. Black tar and speed were exactly what she needed to keep the sharp pain of her daddy between her legs from entering her heart. He had a smell of cheap scotch and scratchy whiskers. It all made her shudder to think of it, so she chased her medicine down the foil, and felt the waves of pain disappear. She stayed at the lake during the day, disappearing now and then for more oxy or tar and scamming some change from the tourists. They'd pay for worms, so stupid. One day her daddy saw she wasn't really in school and that was it. She ran and ran, but he caught her, and at the age of 15 she knew hell like no one should. That night she went into town with all she could carry. After a few days things got blurry, but the heroin held her hand like Jesus used to.

She doesn't like to remember that. She knows that she's not an addict forever like they say in NA. She just had to let Jesus back into her heart. She was sick, so sick for days. The people at the church took care of her, held her, and bathed her when she thought she would die. They fed her, listened to her scream and cry, and finally she was healed; the Enemy was gone, the door opened enough to let Jesus back in.

Now, he holds her hand while she sings.

SHAME MEANS NOTHING

Eighteen makes baby girl a woman

booze makes her happy

coke makes her do whatever *you* want

sometimes there's anger

and just a little bit of shame

Eighteen makes baby girl a woman

cussing makes her tough

short skirts make her sexy

coke makes her do mostly what you want

shame means nothing

when there's a bottle in her hand

Eighteen means freedom

or scars on her wrist

baby girl isn't a woman, just a trampled mess

heart broken, soul open

shame means nothing

when blood's running down her fist.

BEATINGS

Next to my computer on my desk is a post-it note with the words "Dad's Doctor." The rest is blank. I've been given the task of finding out his doctor's name and phone number so that we can call him for ideas. Dad's old and frail and confused and not functioning, and we don't know what to do. He lives far away from us and has few friends. I feel sad and helpless, yet not sad enough to move to where he is to care for him. All that would do is anger him. He was always quick to anger, quick to be hurtful.

I remembered one beating, vividly. I was eight, maybe nine, and the family was living in Egypt, in a huge, 100 year old house. The home was amazing – three foot thick walls and a flat roof with turrets. It had a maid's quarters, where my big sister slept. Huge wooden stairs met a great landing with a giant window – my sister and brother told me that a girl had died in the house, a girl just my age, and if I looked in the window at precisely midnight on the exact night of her death, I would see her dressed in a white gown. I dreamed of this poor girl, and dreamed often of falling down the stairs, only the stairs would turn into a vertical metal tunnel, and I'd try to grasp the walls to slow down my fall, but finally would wake screaming with a thump as I hit the floor of my bedroom. The house had a great garden, filled with mango and guava trees and grape vines. I would play in it for hours, find small corners hidden by leaves where I'd pretend to bake pies and play house by myself. I'd fantasize a perfect home with perfectly happy parents and perfectly nice siblings, while covered in Nile-water-mud.

One late evening I stole my big brother's chocolate that he'd gotten from the food shipment we received monthly from Amsterdam. I was maybe eight...it was chocolate, calling my name. My brother was a hormone-addled teen, and he was pissed. Really no big deal, except that my dad would use any excuse to get angry with my brother...his step-son. My mom defended Geoff; my dad grew angrier; my mom grew frantic. We kids crept upstairs, trying to hide from the drunken bile that was coming out of both their mouths. But then a crash came, and we saw half of a Terry Jacks' album fly out the living room door. My brother bravely ran downstairs, yelling, "Who broke that?!" thinking of course that it had been my father. It turned out to have been my mother, who'd gone more than slightly hysterical.

As she grabbed the heavy, ornate pewter box from the mantle and swung it toward my father, I saw his arms flash...and heard the soft impact of flesh against cartilage and blood spurted, and as I looked up the pewter hit the table, denting it forever, and my mother's nose broke, changing our lives. My siblings fled out the front door, but I had no such luxury, as I was too young for the night streets of Cairo. I grabbed tissue for the blood that seemed to be flooding out of my mother's face and cried, and cried, and cried. Later that night as my mother lay in bed with ice bags on her nose and eyes, my father came in to calm me. I turned away, wishing him dead, staring at the cream colored wall and fading out of my head. His voice: "Please don't cry; no one was hurt." And the fallacy of those words, the chuckle in his voice, the glitter in his eyes, drove me further from him still.

My brother went off to college not too long after the nose-break incident, my sister followed after we'd moved to Norway, and I was left with the drunken pieces of their marriage. I imagined him dead many times...when my mother would pull out maps to help me decide where we would move, where we could move to if only he no longer existed in our world. She, of course, was leaning more toward divorce than murder, but either one would have worked in my mind.

Today I talk to him on the phone; he's over 80, still gruff and short with his words. He never had much to say, unless it was mean. Now he's only mean to my sister or those who bother to care. He hasn't spoken to my brother in 14 years. I can't care anymore, which saddens me, but now his bile doesn't affect me. He's my father, I should be sad that he is so alone and frail. Instead I remember the beatings my mother took, the verbal abuse we all faced daily. He called me a whore and a stupid cunt and a bitch and later others called me that because I thought that was what love meant.

When my mom died, he was there, but he said nothing because he didn't know how. I like to tell people that the day she died was the only time he said "I love you" to me. But frankly, I think I made that up; he never said those words. There was no funeral; there were no tears on his part. We flew back from Mexico with her cremated remains, threw them in the ocean near their home on the Island, and he had a drink.

So...the post-it note on my desk is blank. Tomorrow I will do what a dutiful daughter should do, and I will find out his doctor's name and phone number. But then, because I have no desire to face his wrath, I will try to talk my sister into not calling, into not caring, into letting life run its course on a man whose only legacy will be pain.

LOVE STORY ON PICO

His wife died a few years ago. He sat at our table one
sunny morning and told us the Love story, tender blustery
words over the Pico traffic noise, and we ate our grits
and eggs and listened. The story is written on the menu, but
he needed to tell it to another new stranger-friend. Levis
jacket with the pocket worn thin in Marlboro shape, and he
smiles as he tells of meeting her and their love and struggle and
how finally they bought the place, and then she was gone.

His son, younger but same craggy, rugged not-so-
handsome but comforting face, is behind the register managing all
day and all night. Our favorite waitress, despite the waiting crowd,
listens with patience and a smile to my daughter as she babbles
with excitement to her new friends. Her drawings join others in
the window over time as we become Friday night semi-regulars.
We meet Scott who sits alone but talks to us as he eats enormous
amounts of biscuits and gravy and steak and always his favorite

pie and ice cream and he sells Tumi at the mall and presents me
with his card, proud of his title and gives me tips in case I want to

buy a condo like he did when his mom finally went to the nursing home. The Friday night counter holds quiet regulars who eat and leave, serious in their solitude, always one stool between them.

Saturday mornings it's different; the counter is chatty with neighborhood hunger, and I meet new friends - an ex-cop/body guard whose car is getting fixed across the street, a sweet late-teen girl who glows as she talks of interning in the fashion district. Her dog ate something bad and shit all over her apartment and her roommate was pissed and I remind her of her mom. We see each other weekly and I'm proud of her new job and worried about the dog and...she'll go far in life, sweet sunny Maria.

Before they stopped serving dinner a while back, I took my daughter for an honor-roll treat. He's outside smoking and inside chatting but different, and I watch him, worried. He doesn't talk about his wife much anymore, just superficial and strained jest. Later three young girls come in dressed to go out clubbing, and he hugs them in a certain proprietary way. Blonde and

grungy-chic, smoking outside and then back in, laughing too loud and dressed too skimpy for Pico and La Cienega early Friday evening. And then of course they go to the back with him, purses still at the table and one returns for her phone and they're gone a bit too long and then they're back again glassy eyed and stirring their tea with fast spoons and he's with them too and they talk and talk and he listens and sits and listens, three times their age and gazing off into the distance while they talk and they know they're so interesting and smart and witty and they're young and they'll leave to go dance and maybe call him again in an hour or so and for a moment he'll have pretty girls who pretend to care...

Last weekend I asked why he closes for dinner now. "It's too hard at night in this area, not enough business..." We are standing close and his eyes touch mine and I keep mine there too, and touch his shoulder, "You all right?"

A puzzled flash, but still our eyes meet, and I'm not letting him off easy. And he looks down for just a moment and then back to me, "You know, I've never lived alone before."

SCARS

A small slight circle under my left cheekbone where Caspar the friendly dog bit me when I was perhaps three after I had danced around him as he slept and wanted to let him know how much I loved his sweetness when he had kept me from falling down the stairs by blocking the landing, and so I lifted my skirt to show him my privates, but he didn't respond so I kissed him and startled him out of sleep, and he was old and cranky but would never hurt his baby girl, but still he snarled and bit my cheek, and I screamed, and I saw blood, and my mother freaked out and said that was it, he had to be put to sleep she was sick of him. And the next day when I came home from the park, he was gone.

Discolored odd shapes on both my knees from falling off bikes. Various neighbors in various Calgary suburbs would carry me home and mom would pick out the pebbles as I sat on the edge of the tub and cried. She'd pour peroxide or rubbing alcohol or maybe betadine…it burned like crazy, and then I would grab my knee and the pressure would make more blood come out, and she'd wipe it again and pour more till the blood stopped.

Long pieces of missing skin on my shins from learning to shave my legs. Age 12 and I had no breasts but everyone else was shaving in grade eight, and it was bad enough I had to ask mom for a bra, and she laughed and said they didn't make them that small. She was French, and they didn't make them so small there, and it turned out neither did they in Norway, but my friends from Dallas and Oklahoma had gotten theirs' over summer-break, and I couldn't go to gym class without one. My dad noticed my shaved legs first and yelled at me for being too brazen for 12, and later as the years went on he continued to scream at his baby who was shacking up with everyone in the goddamn country, such a stupid whore (with his Canadian voice and whisky breath it became "hoor" and spit would gather as his face grew red and mom hovered in the background trying to keep out of it so no one would get punched).

Two inch line on the left of my neck; it turns dark pink when I'm tired or stressed. At eighteen I'd been snorting coke for 3 years and the sinus and throat infections just stayed – doc never thought to tell me not to drink or drug on antibiotics and next thing I know they're biopsying for lymphoma, and I'm sure I'll die, but then it's negative, but the incision gets infected and explodes one night on my boyfriend, and I go into shock and end up in ICU for 5 days where they lance my neck twice a day, and I first discover Percocet.

Diagonal lines across the inside of my wrists, the left far deeper than the right. I lived in the freshman dorms for a minute till the photography teacher asked me out to an Animals concert in Philly one night and next moment we were banging it out in his apartment or the darkroom all the time, and I got so angry when I found the naked photos of his ex who was also a redhead, and I imagined if he took naked shots of her and not of me, he must love her more. He thought things I had done made me something evil and definitely a whore. He said I was going to hell because I

47

wasn't accepting Jesus into my life, but finally I had enough of being a hell-whore and had someone buy me whisky and took apart a safety razor and sat in my dorm room and sliced and sliced and sliced. The Resident Assistant was pissed to be awakened to drive me to the ER, and my roommate tried to hit on the Doctor, and the college made me leave, and my mom confessed to me all her suicide attempts, and my dad said I didn't need a shrink because I was just a goddamn stupid hoor who needed to learn a lesson, and the ex-boyfriend told my sister I was possessed by Satan, and she thought that actually might be an option.

A deeper jagged cut across my artery on my left wrist. We always fought, and he was crazy with hallucinations and paranoia when he smoked crack, and I'd already broken a 40 ounce over his head when he raped me, but that night he just wouldn't, wouldn't, wouldn't stop, and I needed to feel something besides the evil bile from his mouth and brain, and so I grabbed a corner of glass from the broken window and sliced just a little, and the blood that spurted out stopped even him for a moment, and we looked at each other in silence, but then he started some more bile, and I wrapped it tight and got a cigarette instead and **burned my palm** over and over and over.

Small whisper of a line across my pelvic area. When I was 18 months sober, she was delivered by emergency C-section after 16 hours of labor and no dilation. My brother and sister photographed it all, and one of them stroked my head as they cut her out of my belly, and they held up the mirror so I could see but the blood and guts made me woozy despite the morphine haze, and they held her up to me, and she was bald and sweet and lovely and looked just like my mother before she died, and I held her little thumb.

Two barely visible half-inch lines on my upper right stomach. I just thought I had bad luck with restaurants and food-poisoning or maybe an ulcer but it never occurred to me to go to a doctor when I was lying on the bathroom floor for days at a time puking up foam and writhing in pain. At 2 years sober I took a chance (you goddamn hoor, stupid hypochondriac, just like your mother…) and went for a physical and a week later they removed my gallbladder through my bellybutton, and I never puked again.

Six different small holes in my right hip, three of them still bright purple, three of them faded to nearly invisible. When the baby was one my hip started hurting, and finally I tried a doctor and then another and yet another, and they said it was nothing, or they said I needed replacement, or they said do sports, or they gave me cortisone. The pain got worse, and I limped all the time, and for a while couldn't even have sex, and the boy I was with gave up, and then so did I, and then someone made me go to someone who knew, and I had arthroscopic surgery and within two days felt better than ever before, but two years later it tore some more, and they did it again but this time **drilled holes in my bones** to try to re-grow cartilage, and now every step hurts and at age 43 I need a new hip.

Two inch vertical slot next to my spine on the back of my neck. A disk ruptured while I worked out, and the next day I went for a job interview on Vicodin, unable to turn to look at the executive asking me questions and certainly unable to smile.

A year later it's re-ruptured and I'm waiting for spinal fusion and yet another **line on the front of my neck**. I will be taken to the hospital by a man who never called me a stupid hoor or a cunt or a bitch, and who has cared for me through two other surgeries and held my hand when I cried in pain before the meds kicked in, and who lets me rest whenever it hurts, and who doesn't think I am possessed and has never tried to rape me, and who loves my daughter as if she were his own, and who sometimes runs his fingers across my scars and loves them because they are mine.

SAME DEATH, DIFFERENT PLACES

He had white hair and grey skin and no top teeth and bits of lung came up when he coughed. He paid the old hooker in crack to give him blowjobs when no one was around. Walter would pound his back when he couldn't breathe. He shoplifted better than anyone I'd ever seen…taillight-sets down his pants and ten videos at a time. Back then it was videos, and sensor razor blades. Those were our big earners. And toothbrushes were easy and sold for a dollar a pop. Eyeliner too, the fancy stuff was more and I'd distract while he shoved thousands of dollars in cosmetics down his pants. Eventually prison won.

She was a pregnant hooker named Kiki who beat her father for his welfare check. He sat in the corner and prayed while she smoked crack and yelled. She'd stolen half a kilo from her ex-boyfriend who then got his legs broken. She lived to tell about it for a bit; he didn't. She had a baby. I saw her in jail. Then she was gone.

Dawn was another hooker, with six inch abscesses on her legs. She covered them strategically. She stole my TV. She wouldn't take her antibiotics and wouldn't let them amputate.

I went to rehab with Jennifer. She had a harder life than most I knew, wrote beautifully and hurt achingly. She married Tracy, and they didn't live happily ever after because Jennifer just couldn't find her way out for long enough.

I barely knew Sasha, but he represented hope to me. His spine hurt worse than mine, which seemed impossible but I saw it in his eyes. I thought he had won.

Same death, different places....

BY NOW

By now
you'd be 8
and if
he weren't so horrendous,
you would be here.

But he stole and lied and raped
and manipulated and beat me.
You wouldn't have lived.

I tore my arms
with a blade, to help
my pain go away.

But did
you feel pain, that moment,
while
I slept,
my feet in stirrups.

I'd tried not to
think about
you at 8.

EL SUPREMO

We met when I was three months along in rehab. The house took us to a meeting in Silver Lake. I was the only straight woman in a group of 15 women. I fancied myself better than them all, not because of my sexual preference, but simply because before I became a crack-head I had gotten a good education and a glamorous job in the film biz. The fact that we were all recovering addicts and alcoholics and that I had spent more cumulative time in jail than most of the other women didn't cross my mind then. I was better and different and refined and cosmopolitan. I had travelled the world and dated a millionaire and attended film festivals and worn designer clothes and read the classics. When I was in jail I re-read *The Grapes of Wrath* not the Harlequin romances the other girls preferred. Really, didn't all that matter far more than the fact that I had once gone to a motel room with my hooker friend because she had a client that needed to be diapered and he would pay us both good money and furnish lots of crack?

And so when we went to this AA meeting in the Silver Lake hills in a pretty old house that was ram-shackle and faded, I saw the hummingbirds and the gay men in a sort of *Breakfast at Tiffany's* light. He approached me immediately. My red-hair was long, and before rehab I had already finished four months in jail and was starting to gain weight and look good again. He spoke with that exact enunciation perfected by old movie stars from the 1950s. His R's rolled beautifully, and he took my arm and me charmed with his beautiful manners and the words of a well-educated man. He called me beautiful and brought me tea and quoted lovely poetry and classic literature. We spoke at length, and when he discovered I had lived and travelled in Europe, Asia and the Middle East, he spoke knowingly of Islam and Buddhism and whispered lovely French verses in my eager ear. I had been apart from knowledge and refinery for so long, entrenched in the street and the underground of Echo Park. To me he was a delightful fresh breath. He said he was a conductor and taught violin and took young kids from the street to play in a Symphony.

Oh, but I was charmed. I would call him from the payphone in the gritty hall of the rehab, and he would play me Bach and Mozart on his violin and recite Kahlil Gibran, and Buddha, and Jesus as well. He said he would take me to see a symphony downtown, and when I reminded him I had no clothes, (having lost everything I owned to crack), he said he would buy me whatever I wanted. The counselors at the center said absolutely not; and I cried. They asked why I thought an old man would do this for me, and I naively and quite sincerely replied that he was just a sweet old gay man who had no interest in women, particularly ones as young as I.

When I graduated from the program, he came with one of his young male "sponsees" and he spoke during the ceremony. I thought that his perfect timbre and enunciation and charm bewildered the women in the home. Many were from the streets of East LA, and I was sure they didn't know what to make of him. My friend Lorraine said I should be careful but wouldn't explain and retreated when I defended him. He helped me to move to the small sober-living house. I had no car, and he would drive me to and fro so that I wouldn't have to take the bus.

When I finally saw where he lived, the weekend after my graduation, I was surprised. It was near my old neighborhood where I'd squatted in an abandoned building and smoked crack, but a bit further east and, I rationalized, in the "hills." Well, the foothills. It was a small single apartment, crammed with artifacts and rugs and tapestries from the Middle East and Mexico and Europe. His kitchen was dirty but the walls were covered in photos of Peter at various ages, next to famous people, next to beautiful women, next to beautiful men. Violins hung everywhere, a speaker blared classical music, there were Buddhas and Marys and large blue Evil Eyes and small writing in Hebrew, and a picture of him – a picture of Peter with the words, "El Supremo," carefully lettered in calligraphy underneath.

We had tea and some sweet breads and fresh tamales from the bakery down the street. I finally asked his last name, as I had no concept at all of where he might be from. And, to my surprise, out rolled a very Spanish last name. He told me bits and pieces of his life, growing up in East Los Angeles. He spoke of two wives and his children who no longer contacted him. How he had almost 20 years sober. When it was time for me to go home, he drove me back, forever calling me *mi amore* and holding my hand. I found it just a sweet charming mannerism from an eccentric man, and left it at that. He would kiss my cheeks and end with a lingering kiss on my lips.

When he asked me to marry him, I thought certain that he was teasing. I laughed and moved on to another topic. And yet he wouldn't let it go. I had found I was pregnant, and the father wanted nothing to do with me, despite having known him for fourteen years and having dated him for months since I'd gotten sober. Peter asked if I would live with him, marry him, I was his true love and reminded him so of his first wife. He told me tales of them running through America and Mexico and Europe; his life seemed like a Hemingway novel. I asked him why his children still wouldn't talk to him, but he always changed the subject.

At times Peter would phone me twenty times a day. I would be napping – the pregnancy was hard both emotionally and physically. His messages were those of a petulant young lover,

combined with years of practice at manipulation. He brought me soup and crackers and drove me to AA meetings. He brought sweet blankets for the baby when she arrived. He spoke of his young male "sponsees" who needed a place to stay and so he let them stay on his couch in exchange, as he put it, for a little help around the house. He took them to the park for meditation, he gave them bits of money, they, "took advantage," he said. These youngsters never stayed sober for long. They would move out in a huff and stop calling him. He would find a new one, and then his calls to me would cease for a week or so. At AA meetings he would share eloquently – but to me, finally, his words went from sounding so wise and sincere and filled with compassion to trite and pompous and so hypocritical.

And yet still he was there – he helped me care for my daughter at times, he brought food, he brought medicine when I was sick. He thanked me for brightening the world of a foolish old man, and despite myself, there were times when I couldn't resist the charm. We drove through Griffith Park and waved madly at hikers and

picnickers and laughed and cheered and then as the sun darkened listened quietly to the concerto on the radio, and I let him hold my hand while my daughter slept in the back seat.

Often months or more would pass without me being able to face his calls. He'd send letters in strong yet delicate calligraphy, always signed "El Supremo" Sometimes he'd enclose tickets to the Hollywood Bowl or the Dorothy Chandler Pavilion. I'd go, often alone, and sit with him while he basked in the music. His tears would slide through closed lids.

One day he called me to meet him on Olvera Street – I must meet Paloma. And there, in a small restaurant with loud mariachis, was a beautiful young 20-something, exotic girl. She had long lush wavy hair and such red lips and a smile that touched heaven. He gushed over her, called her name with pride, and we shook hands and hugged, and his eyes were so alive. The violinist came to the table, and Peter and Paloma sang loudly and beautifully in Spanish. For months after, his calls and letters were filled with stories of Paloma. And then she disappeared, as so many young people did from his world. Again, he was at my door with bits of food and the phone rang too often and the messages left were sad and manipulative and set me off in a fury.

Others at AA meetings would mention him, some deriding his "sponsee-ship" of the young men, others speaking only with love and kindness. He wanted to teach my daughter violin, but after a couple of afternoons at his apartment with her young tiny hands in his and his arms around her, I grew nervous with thoughts of his children who still wouldn't contact him, and so I faded away again.

It had been almost two years since I'd seen him. The phone rang, and an unknown number appeared; and for once I took a chance and answered. Peter was on the other end, his voice soft and raspy, and he said he had to move, and he was sick with cancer, and he'd been at the VA all week for chemo, and he would love to see me and my little one. And somehow this time it didn't sound quite so manipulative, and there was fear in his voice; and so we went.

His "sponsee" was supposed to be helping him pack, along with another young man to whom he taught violin. The apartment was

a wreck – dirty and dusty and chaotic with boxes, no semblance of any kind of order. There was little food in the fridge, and the sink was filthy. Peter struggled out of his chair, and I saw that the rotund bear of a man had become a whisper of flesh. His false teeth made his smile too big, but still the twinkle was in his eyes. My name rolled off his tongue as he hugged me to him, and I felt only bones beneath the layers of clothes. My daughter stood wide-eyed; I'd explained in the car that this man she had known for 8 years was now dying and that was why we had to go visit. He hugged her tight, and for once I felt no fear as I watched. He talked and talked, an old vulnerable man clinging to shreds of his old life. He showed me magazines and violins and an old cello and told the stories behind them. The people helping him pack were useless and kept asking for food and money. Peter would not let me help, but after a time I stood and started in the kitchen. My daughter was good and didn't complain and finally fell asleep on his old stained couch, where I knew many a young "sponsee" had stayed. Peter walked the small apartment, picking up bits of his life, moving them to a box or a bag. Various people came by,

mostly for money, none to help. I asked after Paloma, and he said she called now and then. His plan was to have his son move out and care for him in an assisted living home…but the paperwork was taking a long time and so for now he was putting his life in storage and would find some place to stay. I was surprised and happy to hear that his son was talking to him finally after so many years...apparently he'd met his grandson and indeed even his great-grandson.

Just weeks later, on the anniversary of his 29th year sober, I picked him up from a small boarding house in East Hollywood. He used a cane and had a small oxygen tank. I took him to his favorite AA meeting, where he proudly and eloquently accepted a cake. He spoke to the crowd, said he planned to be around in 3 months to give me a cake to celebrate my 10 years of sobriety. He said it would keep him alive, and I was quietly moved to tears.

A week before my 10 year anniversary, Peter called me with a weak and faded voice. He was moving to Arizona – his family would care for him while he died. He'd spent the last few weeks

living in cheap hotels on Hollywood Blvd...his latest "sponsee" had taken his money and left; the VA had failed to cure his cancer and the government paperwork proved too complicated and arduous a process to find him a decent place to die in dignity. In contradiction to his earlier stories about his son caring for him, he told me that an old friend in Palm Desert had seen him and secretly called his family. They finally had agreed to bring him home. He would not be in town to give me a 10-year AA cake. Prideful, I wondered how he would stay alive.

A month after he left Los Angeles, three weeks after I turned 10 years sober, the phone rang. "El Supremo's" frail and faded voice, leaving a raspy and sad message...

CLEAN SOULS

i

There is a stir in the air, could be rain (for the first time in months). A newspaper flies across my window, driven by the wind to the street below. Letters, strewn upon the street now, paragraphs of people's lives that were read yesterday and forgotten today. Cars pass by (too quickly, too loud), through my life in a flash of lights. A man walks below, slowly, drunken, muttering out loud but his words are lost to the wind. He stumbles and falls, but nobody stops to help. I watch from above, as the first drops of rain hit his face and he struggles to lift himself up and away. His face is twisted and wrinkled. He looks in my window, as he adjusts his matted clothes. His eyes meet mine.

And the rain begins now, hard and driving. It will cleanse the air. It will cleanse our souls. I close the window, shutting out the drops and the stare of the man. My breath leaves a ring of fog.

ii

Outside the desert looks hot and inviting, but inside I feel the cold. I've sat wrapped in a blanket for hours, unwilling to move. An icy breeze comes through the window. It tickles my nose. I do not stir. The coyote and I have been staring at each other for what seems like days. Perhaps he cannot see me? I watch him stand unmoving in my yard. He is alone. He is very old. Mangy. He reminds me of something from the past, something I cannot place. He looks toward the window now and then, and sniffs the air. He frightens me.

The sun is starting to go down, and the cold is getting unbearable, but I cannot make myself move to turn on the heat. I have cleared my mind. I watch the lone coyote, and I do not think. The darkness settles over my chair. The coyote starts to lie down on the cold ground. I wonder what he is waiting for.

In the morning I awaken in the same position. My neck is stiff, and the air comes out of my mouth in a cloud of steam. The sun has risen over the desert outside my windows, and the colors fill me. I look for my coyote but he is gone, vanished into the vista.

There is not a living thing to be seen, just cactus in the distance. Does it have a soul?

My blanket scratches my face, and I force myself to stand, creaking with the effort. I turn on the heat. I use the toilet. I look at the lines on my face in the mirror. I eat some bread. And then I go back to my window. He is there, looking at me from the yard, his color blending with the yellow-brown of the sand. Finally he sits on the ground with his back to me, and I sit in my chair.

At noon he leaves, giving me a parting glance, and I wonder where he feeds. I fill the bath with hot water and lower myself in. I have managed not to think for nearly two days now. I watch the bubbles form around my nipples and push all memories away. The water finally becomes cold, and I rub myself with a rough towel, not looking. I put on fresh long-johns and return to the window. But he has not returned.

The next day I let myself start to read a book, but it brings thoughts with its words, and I must put it down. I wait, staring out the glass, but the coyote never comes back. I clean the cabin. I cook a pot of soup and watch it boil for hours. I picture bodies in the broth, rolling with the vegetables. I try to remember cars, different makes, different years, but they all seem the same in my mind. They are all green. I try to recall if I ever knew anyone with a green car, but no one comes to mind. I don't let myself think about it for long. Memories can be dangerous.

Yesterday I thought I saw snow, but I am in a cabin in the desert. I know there was ice on the window, because I touched it with my tongue, feeling it stick for just an instant, tasting the flat taste, feeling the moisture melt with my body heat.

iii

The mountain snow has been falling since this morning, and I have stood at the window, watching, wrapped in my sweater. A blanket is falling on the earth, shutting out all sounds. It is dark now, the electricity out. I have surrounded myself with candles, lit

a small fire (flames to watch, blue forever). Blankets drape me, soft to touch. The window is huge, and I watch the world turn white.

The silence becomes noise, and I listen to it, waiting to hear just a sound out of place. I am alone. The wind begins, hurling flakes at the building. I look at the cars under their white covering (but cars have no souls). Perhaps it is over, and I am to be alone on this earth, surrounded by cold and blinding white. Perhaps I have died and this is the limbo I must learn to live in.

I touch my hand to the window and lift it to see the print left behind. The sharpness of the cold sends a shiver down my spine. I see the snow, brushing the window more gently now, the wind soft. It caresses the glass. I want to feel that touch on my skin. I take off my clothes in the dark of the room, the light of the candles and the fire lighting me red and blue. The snow touches the pane, and I press my naked body to the glass, letting the flakes melt in to my skin.

IN MY ARMS

When she was born, and they put her in my arms, traces of morphine from the c-section still clouded my mind and I saw her sweet little bald head and the sharp jaw-line, the same as my mother right before she died. My mother, the bald head and the bruises around her eyes from the accident in the cancer center, that damn clinic in Tijuana, they really had no idea what they were doing, and then the pain that she felt, and watching me with those eyes, the same huge eyes that my daughter has now, dark brown and so full of love and trust and a little misunderstanding, a little bit of confusion, *why is the pain so bad and how much longer must I be here on this earth*, but my mother can no longer talk, only hold my hand, and there is blood on her gums and then when she is gone I see only emptiness, still. I never rid that image from my mind, the empty shell they wheeled past me as I sat alone in the early morning lobby of that clinic, smell of old coffee and a squeak of the gurney, her body shrouded like they did with Jesus, but she didn't even believe in a god.

And me, between not believing in God, and then believing but hating him; knowing that I wanted to be with her and the only way I could was to die too, to end the pain, to leave this world where so much hurt happened every day. I tried to leave my mind, leave my body and spirit. I cried, I hurt, I drugged, I drank, I escaped in words, in books, in dreams, in music, into hate, but found only more pain and then the drugs didn't help and she was still there; every time I closed my eyes I saw the specks of blood on her gums, the hollow shell, the empty eyes. I tried not to sleep, woke screaming and crying when I did, stayed up for days, smoked more drugs till I couldn't tell if I were awake or asleep or if those demons were real or in my head. And God couldn't have found me if he'd tried, because I had hidden so well, forced all thought out, forced all dreams to end, all hope to die, all love to turn away, and there was no way up anymore.

When someone tells you enough times that you're a stupid bitch, a cunt, a whore, if they rape you enough and hurt you enough, soon it doesn't matter anymore; they are right and you are wrong and to escape is pointless. There isn't escape -- the pain won't leave, the drugs only last a moment, no one is there. I still looked for her. I still looked for God, just once in a while, late in the night after no one was awake, when the stars almost looked real again and I could almost remember her voice and her touch. And I would sleep for a moment, haunted by the fact that I could never get back, that I was so low I would never rise again, and yet I couldn't fucking die.

Others around me died, rotting in their rooms till someone thought to call a cop. We'd take the things we could use and leave the rest to the families, if they could be found. The yellow tape on the door didn't stop us, we needed a place to sleep, some warmth for the night, and their ghosts were already in us anyway.

When Chief went I wasn't surprised, except that it had taken so long. He'd really died long ago, as most of us had. He would nod, talking to himself, seeing evil spirits and hallucinating for hours. He became convinced I was really a man since I wouldn't fuck him; truly certain in his mind that I couldn't be a woman. He smelled of crack and sickly-sweet heroin and sweat and had bigger breasts than I did. His wife had left him for a woman, and he'd call her name over and over while he nodded. Sometimes he thought I was her and would yell at me, and I feared he would hit me, but then he'd snap back and remind me what a cunt I was and why wouldn't I at least suck him just once, he'd give me a dime, maybe two if I would, please just once, but I would leave to my apartment below, listening to him thumping and tapping the floor all night, till he fell over hard and I'd go check on him. The smell of gas would come under the door, and I'd break in again, save his life again, one more time so he would be able to steal with me the next day so I could get just a little more crack, one more day, just one more day and then I'll quit. When he got busted outside K-mart I ran, let them take him away. He got out, months later, I knew. But this time I stayed away, I hid from him and his evil and his hatred. When he died, I felt relief, was ashamed of the joy I felt for a moment when I learned that truly the most evil person I had ever known was finally gone. But now I hold my daughter in my arms and think, he was someone's child once too...someone loved him, held him, just like this. His mother tried to bring charges against the girl who'd supplied the drugs, but of course there was no proof, and we didn't have to tell her that the suicide-letter was real. The way he lived was proof enough, and it couldn't have lasted, no matter what she wanted to believe.

I believed Tom's words and his lies when I met him, felt his touch and believed there was good. He was so ill, and somehow I felt that if I could hold him while he died, stay till he went, maybe it would bring me closer to my mother's ghost, closer to my destiny, closer to God? His cough was just like hers before she left, that night I held her for so many hours and she stared at me, hard, trying to speak but no words could escape the pain and terror. Finally I slept and so she left me, her eyes empty and still, the fear gone, and I held her foot, couldn't touch her hand, my dad took off her ring, put it on my finger but one day I would sell that too, just to get another moment of escape, another breath of smoke.

To be with a dying thief seemed like a better alternative to me than the abusive fiancé, and so I stayed with Tom, cared for him as I had for her, pounded his back and chest when he couldn't breath, helped him bathe and helped him steal, cooked our drugs and brought him more. When my fiancé broke in and beat us both, screaming with anger and hatred and wanting revenge and drugs, I fought him off and held Tom as the blood came to his lips, gasping, broken, and carried him away to help. He lived through that, lived to steal more and smoke more, but after Christmas we were caught and they took him away, to die not in my arms but in a prison up north.

Jim was a junkie lost in a dream of his old life; he stayed in our hotel-room while we were waiting for Tom to die, and we used his van, bringing him dope as he got sick, and food now and then. He spent hours looking at photos of his wife and the three daughters who waited for him in Whittier while he shot up on Olympic and Douglas, thinner by the day, nodding over his crack pipe and trying to find a vein. He'd miss and the rig would hit the dirty floor, pick it up and try again and again and again. I didn't want him to shoot up in front of me, but he'd take so long to find a spot and he'd nod and forget and finally once he nodded while standing in front of the toilet and fell and destroyed the whole thing, along with some ribs. We paid off the management and they let us stay, we nursed him along for weeks, taking his car while he lay in bed in pain, dope sick and ribs broken, coughing and smoking and shooting while we drove all over town stealing Tylenol, razor blades, batteries and car parts. When we got arrested they took the van too, and Jim was left still waiting, sicker and sicker while we sat in jail and they destroyed his car, looking for guns and more evidence than they already had. Recorded our conversation while we sat in the back of the cop car, me crying hysterically because I knew Tom would die, knew they'd take him to prison, and we tried to work out a story but there was no saving him, no deals to be made this time. Jim died in a motel about a year later...he'd cleaned up, went home to wife and daughters, but came back for one more run. Met a little Hispanic hooker who used to shoot up in her neck, using car mirrors to get it just right...she wouldn't tell him she loved him, she left him alone in the room for hours one day, though he begged her to stay, said he couldn't live without her, wouldn't live...

This morning my daughter runs her small, soft fingers over the scars on my arms. I dread the day that she finally asks. He would yell at me for hours, over and over, days and days until the pain of the glass against flesh felt better than his words...up for days he would think there were cameras in the ceiling and people under the floor and that I was letting them fuck me while he smoked another hit. The burn of a cigarette deep into my skin, apartment cold with no electricity or gas, rain coming down outside and through the broken window, mice hiding in our clothes and roaches looking for crumbs, and I would burn and burn, try to get him to stop, make the words end, go away, just leave me in peace and quiet and a haze of smoke. He'd rape me and I broke a bottle over his head, didn't even phase him for more than a moment, traces of blood around the ears as he yelled more hatred, then coming back and pleading for some love and more to smoke. I wanted to beat him till he stopped, break his head and his heart, make him feel the pain he brought me, but I only brought it to myself over and over and over, letting him back in again...

I tried to help Debbie. She was a hooker lived mostly under the bridge of the Alvarado freeway exit. Shot heroin into her leg muscles, would only give head since she had abscesses on both legs at least 6 inches in diameter; couldn't remember to take her antibiotics and wouldn't go to the hospital because they spoke of amputating. Asked me what was wrong, why I didn't like to be touched, wouldn't let anyone hug me...she couldn't understand that all those who touched died or hurt me in the end, better not to let them in. I let her stay in my room, take a shower and dye her hair, sleep in warmth. She propositioned the old man next door, stole my key and came back later for my stuff. I expect she's dead now too, legs rotted away until the toxins killed her.

Red lived in a cave under the 101 freeway at the Alvarado Street exit bridge. He'd fixed it up with old rugs and drapes and bits of candle. Two or three could fit in there real nice, as long as we'd all bathed recently or were covered enough not to smell.

Jerry could never come in; his feet smelled so bad no one would let him near, tweaking away as he walked; he got beat up by the cholos after robbing them too many times, never made it back to the freeway, but we all knew. Red cleans windows at the gas station, I see him still. He remembers me, I always give him money and food and he tells me how proud he is. Walter too, though I haven't seen him in years, since my daughter was born and he couldn't believe it was my girl I carried down the street; he drove right by me, didn't recognize me with some weight and sunshine in my eyes. He held me in his arms once, bathed the sweat off my face while I coughed and coughed, pneumonia infecting my lungs but no one believed, wouldn't take me to the hospital; and then I awakened naked on the motel room carpet, covered in sweat and coughing over and over and over and finally cried for help and they called a cab, dropped me at the ER door. I stayed five days and left to get high, bruises from the IV's on my hands and arms, couldn't hardly hold in the smoke, but it felt so good to get out and be high again, till finally one day I sat in that jail cell and couldn't cry anymore and felt her holding me tight and telling me I'd be ok; till I found her in the darkness of the night, a small skylight window lighting the cell bars, and my mother's soul finally surrounded me. And when the E.P.T. came back positive, how could I not keep her, and the first time I held her in my arms, how could I not see those eyes, so huge and dark and trusting with just a little bit of confusion, and only love.

SEEING MEMORIES

I can't see my memories since we left LA...

Lankershim south of Ventura Boulevard was Brian and my house was the guest house behind his house. And somehow one night we ended up together after Micelli's and too much beer. And then months went by and I'd break out in hives before every date. He took my breath away, he had my soul, but he dumped me because, "he didn't want a commitment." And then he married *HER* three months later. He came by on the way to his wedding, drunk, to tell me he loved me and he was making a huge mistake, and he left as I stood in the door sobbing.

On Vine St. was the Hollywood Palace and coke off the bar; Kevin would be on acid again, so we'd all leave and go to my guest house. and I'd read bad poetry to the boys who wanted just my body and not my soul.

First we'd go to the Firefly where I had dated the bartender who set the bar on fire every night to a packed house of drunks grooving on the jukebox, and the dealer sat in the front corner, while we did lines off the toilet. When the Firefly shut down we all moved to Boardner's on Cherokee because the Frolic Room was a bit too ghetto for our dealer. George the bartender had been in "Taxi" and gave me free drinks, and there was this tall fellow who took me to a lovely dinner but I just wanted coke at the time, not men...since Brian left I'd stopped giving my soul. Later when I became a crackhead I wouldn't go to bars in case someone recognized me, and also it was too expensive. That's when Santa Monica and Vermont Avenue became my home, a squat a block away from the Community College and up the street from the School for the Blind. I saw them all walking holding hands while I waited for my dealer, and laughed at the blind leading the blind. But I was blind and didn't know I was standing next to Rena B., a rehab center a block away from my squat, and they all laughed at me when I asked for a quarter for the phone because they knew it was for my dealer, #69 was his taxi number. He drove a cab full of hookers and crack And in the daytime it was #18 who had the number 18 tattooed on his chin because he was an 18th Street gang-banger, and I'd steal baby clothes and diapers for him and his girl who'd just had a baby. I'd ask for credit every night and then steal all day to cover my bills.

El Pollo Loco was good for napkins that I used for toilet paper so I could save money for crack. My neighbor heard voices and drank all day and drank all night and threatened to call the DEA on the other dealer who lived across the road. They tried to get me to suck them off for crack, but I just stole more batteries and pregnancy tests to sell down in Echo Park. Their crack sucked anyway, to hell with them. I was a Booster, not a Whore.

McArthur Park was scary at night, and sometimes I'd take a cab and piss off the drivers who never bought my, "I'm picking up a friend," story. They knew I was scoring, but fuck them, they got their money.

Then there was Tom who died in prison, but he's in another story and I don't like to remember him anymore. Then Willy, whose leg was rotting and abscessed and foul, but he had a car so I paid him in crack to drive me to steal, but then he got greedy, so I fired him and started taking the bus.

That's when James moved in ("I'm the guest that will never leave," hell, was that right!) and we'd scream and yell at each other all night. Then he'd go break into cars and steal stereos at night, and in the day *I'd* boost, and then we'd smoke and then we'd fight, and that was really the beginning of the end.

Then there was Twin Towers County Jail, and I could never drive by there without remembering the cavity searches, and the food and the girls who punched me. But then there were the ones who had my back, and I slept a lot and tried to gain weight – 99lbs isn't pretty when you're 5'8". And then McArthur Park became a new memory of rehab and recovery – Alcoholism Center for Women was right across the street from my old wholesale dealer who'd give you a 20 dollar rock for 10, and now there I was reading Steps 1-3.

I'd see Kiki from my bedroom window, turning tricks pregnant and I'd be reading my morning meditation. I fell in love with Tracy, who years later became Leroy, so maybe that means I was never a lesbian, I don't know. But I graduated proudly days before Christmas and moved back to Echo Park, a sober-living house in the hills with coyotes outside and serenity inside.

Then it was Elvis's birthday and I was on the Sunset Strip with an old flame, holding hands at the House of Blues and then he played and I watched him, proud, and then weeks later I was holding an EPT that I didn't steal, and he said let's get another one to be sure, but neither of us could afford it. *It was* sure, and he was gone. And I kept taking the bus to work in the Valley, Echo Park to Alvarado, and there would be Walter still trying to score, and I was proud of my sobriety and he was too.

Then another bus to Sherman Oaks and finally my boss figured out I was pregnant and didn't fire me, as I'd feared. I came back from having my sweet baby and they made me VP of something. And I was given a car by my old landlord, after I made amends to him and then I was living back on Santa Monica & Vermont Avenue, next to the best Middle Eastern restaurant in all of LA, and the lady next door played Shakira and screamed at her five kids in Spanish, and I yelled at her in English because it was not easy being a single mom and VP and sober, but it was wonderful and I created good memories in East Hollywood to replace the bad ones.

Then a year later I moved to Pico and Fairfax, where my baby had a yard and I had a two-bedroom place, and at night we danced to the blues. And she smiled and laughed and lit up my life.

Then there was Betty, the best daycare I could find, she was old and fabulous and right near the Beverly Center, and I couldn't drive down Beverly without remembering her love. She had one cigarette and a small drink after the kids left every day, and she talked of Boston and how her sister had burned to death on the 4th of July, when a sparkler caught her nightie on fire.

And then my baby Sophia started school and Betty got Alzheimer's, and was placed in a home on Olympic that smelled of urine and old milk, I hated visiting her and seeing her that way. And then she passed away and my heart will always hold her.

Summertime brought the beach and sand castles and waves and pools and a little sunburn. And then I bought a house in Crenshaw where we were the only white people for miles, but it was amazing and gorgeous and art deco and the neighbors were awesome. We got robbed five times and I almost left but then they caught the robbers and I felt safe again.

Then there was Howard who stole all my money when he told me he was a contractor and he destroyed my house, but then Oscar and Miguel put it back together, which seemed like it took forever but it looked amazing, and Miguel asked me out and I had to tell him no, so he stopped doing things for free, but that was ok too. One time my Indian Food delivery guy came over with frilly clothes for Sophia and asked me out and I had to tell him no too, and then I couldn't order Indian food anymore, and I thought maybe I was too nice to people but what could I do, I was a recovering addict who was filled with the sunshine of recovery.

I stayed VP of things at different companies, and bought a different car, and the memories that I drove by became happy and drug free and filled with people like Betty and also Darby and Marilyn who'd stood by me through the drug-years, but stayed away too. And now they were back and they were married and I wasn't, but I had a baby and they didn't, so it was hard, but our friendship lasted through years to come. They were Los Feliz and Silver Lake and Franklin and Talmadge and traffic jams and great food and love.

Then it was Jason and Culver City and sunshiny music and his smile that lit up the world, but he didn't want to be a dad, so he went away. And then one afternoon there was an email from Brian. *That Brian*, the one from Lankershim. And there I was in an office on Sunset, VP of something, and my assistant was babbling and all I could think of was reading that email. He said he was divorced these 17 years later, and wanted to talk with me. So I waited five minutes and called and then it turned out he was sober too, and he had 4 kids, and he came over one night with the youngest and we made a cake while the kids played (is that what sober people do?) and he made amends and I tried not to let him and I was nervous and he looked amazing and I remembered all our times together. Weeks went by and we chatted and we were cute and one day I almost kissed him but then I turned around and left and then we went out on a date to an AA meeting, what dorks, and then we started dating and then we moved in together and I rented my Crenshaw house to a crazy woman who lied to me and I believed her and she got me for $6k and fled and so I had to short-sell the house and I cried. And Brian's ex made our life a bit hellish because she was crazy and money-grubbing and I called the cops on her once and the kids kinda hated me, but then he asked me to marry him on camera – we were filming some stupid reality show because we lived in LA and that's what Angelinos do -- and he proposed in the final scene and all 7 of us cried, kids and all, and then we got married on the beach in Venice, and the clouds parted as we said our vows (who gets married in March on the beach?!) and it was lovely and even my Dad was there, and then we moved to Tennessee.

And now...I can't see my memories when I drive. But they will always be with me, because just like my scars, the memories, the good and the bad, have all brought me to where I am now.

Nadia uses grains of her often, gritty life to infuse her stories with cathartic realism. Her stories "Fire" and "Scars" have both been finalists in *Glimmer Train's* writing contests and are included here in *SCARS,* her first anthology from Punk Hostage Press. Nadia Bruce-Rawlings grew up travelling the world and living in various countries before settling in Los Angeles. In LA she briefly worked at a vitamin factory and then began a long career in independent film distribution. A single mom for 11 years, she and her new husband have settled into the Nashville area, where she writes by the lake when she can escape their five kids and two dogs.

OTHER PUNK HOSTAGE PRESS BOOKS

FRACTURED (2012) by Danny Baker

BETTER THAN A GUN IN A KNIFE FIGHT (2012)
by A. Razor

THE DAUGHTERS OF BASTARDS (2012) by Iris Berry

*DRAWN BLOOD: COLLECTED WORKS FROM
D.B.P.LTD., 1985-1995* (2012) by A. Razor

IMPRESS (2012) by C.V.Auchterlonie

*TOMORROW, YVONNE - POETRY & PROSE FOR
SUICIDAL EGOISTS* (2012) by Yvonne De la Vega

BEATEN UP BEATEN DOWN (2012) by A. Razor

MIRACLES OF THE BLOG: A SERIES (2012)
by Carolyn Srygley--Moore

8TH & AGONY (2012) by Rich Ferguson

SMALL CATASTROPHES IN A BIG WORLD (2012)
by A. Razor

UNTAMED (2013) by Jack Grisham

MOTH WING TEA (2013) by Dennis Cruz

HALF-CENTURY STATUS (2013) by A. Razor

SHOWGIRL CONFIDENTIAL (2013) by Pleasant Gehman

BLOOD MUSIC (2013) by Frank Reardon

I WILL ALWAYS BE YOUR WHORE/LOVE SONGS for Billy Corgan (2014) by Alexandra Naughton

A HISTORY OF BROKEN LOVE THINGS (2014)
by SB Stokes

YEAH, WELL... (2014) by Joel Landmine

DREAMS GONE MAD WITH HOPE (2014) by S.A. Griffin

CODE BLUE: A LOVE STORY (2014) by Jack Grisham

HOW TO TAKE A BULLET AND OTHER SURVIVAL POEMS (2014) by Hollie Hardy

DEAD LIONS (2014) by A.D. Winans

STEALING THE MIDNIGHT FROM A HANDFUL OF DAYS (2014) by Michele McDannold

WHEN I WAS A DYNAMITER (2014)
by Lee Quarnstrom

FORTHCOMING BOOKS ON PUNK HOSTAGE PRESS

THUGNESS IS A VIRTUE (2014) by Hannah Wehr

WHERE THE ROAD LEADS (2015) by Diana Rose

SHOOTING FOR THE STARS IN KEVLAR (2015)
by Iris Berry

LONGWINDED TALES OF A LOW PLAINS DRIFTER (2015)
by A. Razor

EVERYTHING IS RADIANT BETWEEN THE HATES (2015)
by Rich Ferguson

*GOOD GIRLS GO TO HEAVEN, BAD GIRLS GO
EVERYWHERE* by Pleasant Gehman (2015)

BOULEVARD OF SPOKEN DREAMS (2015) by Iris Berry

DANGEROUS INTERSECTIONS (2015) by Annette Cruz

DRIVING ALL OF THE HORSES AT ONCE (2015)
by Richard Modiano

DISGRACELAND (2015)
by Iris Berry & Pleasant Gehman

AND THEN THE ACID KICKED IN (2015)
by Carlye Archibeque

BODIES: BRILLIANT SHAPES (2015) by Kate Menzies

BORROWING SUGAR (2015) by Susan Hayden

BASTARD SONS OF ALPHABET CITY (2015) by Jon Hess

*THE REDHOOK GIRAFFE & OTHER BROOKLYN
TALES* (2015) by James A. Tropeano III

IN THE SHADOW OF THE HOLLYWOOD SIGN (2015)
by Iris Berry

PURO PURISMO (2015) by A. Razor

SIRENS (2015) by Larry Jaffe